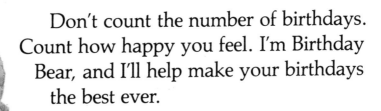

Don't count the number of birthdays. Count how happy you feel. I'm Birthday Bear, and I'll help make your birthdays the best ever.

I'm Wish Bear, and if you wish on my star, maybe your special dream will come true.

If you're ever feeling lonely, just call on me, Friend Bear. See, I've got a daisy for you and a daisy for me.

Grr! I'm Grumpy Bear. There's a cloud on my tummy to show that I take the grouchies away, so you can be happy again.

I'm Love-a-Lot Bear. I have two hearts on my tummy. One is for you; the other is for someone you love.

It's my job to bring you sweet dreams. I'm Bedtime Bear, and right now I'm a bit sleepy. Are you sleepy, too?

Now that you know all of us, we hope that you'll have a special place for us in your heart, just like we do for you.

With love from all of us,

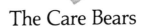

The Care Bears

Published in the United States by Parker Brothers, Division of CPG Products Corp.

Care Bears, Care Bears Logo, Tenderheart Bear, Friend Bear, Grumpy Bear, Birthday Bear, Cheer Bear, Bedtime Bear, Funshine Bear, Love-a-Lot Bear, Wish Bear and Good Luck Bear are trademarks of American Greetings Corporation, Parker Brothers, authorized user.

Library of Congress Cataloging in Publication Data: Johnson, Ward. Ben's new buddy. A Tale from the Care Bears. SUMMARY: Ben gets advice from the Care Bears when his happiness at starting third grade is marred by the class bully.
[1. Bears—Fiction. 2. Schools—Fiction. 3. Bullies—Fiction] I. Title. II. Series.
PZ7.J6394Be 1984 [E] 83-22145 ISBN 0-910313-16-4
Manufactured in the United States of America 2 3 4 5 6 7 8 9 0

A Tale from the
Care Bears

Ben's New Buddy

Story by Ward Johnson
Pictures by Tom Cooke

It was Monday, the first day of a new school year.
Ben and his friend, Fred, walked together. Ben was
wearing his favorite cap, and he felt excited. The first
day of school always seemed special.

"I hope that we both get Mr. Todd," Fred said.
"Everyone knows that he is the best teacher in the
whole school."

"I bet third grade is really going to be neat," Ben
answered.

Ben and Fred went into the schoolyard. They saw many of their friends. Everyone talked about what had happened over summer vacation. Then the bell rang, and all the boys and girls crowded into school.

"Great," said Ben as he glanced quickly at the list
of names outside room 10. "We did get Mr. Todd.
Now I know this is going to be the best year yet."

Mr. Todd came in and began to call the roll. When he called, "Steve Wooly," Fred gave a little groan.

"What's the matter?" Ben asked.

"Don't you know about Steve Wooly?" Fred whispered. "He's the toughest kid in school. He's supposed to be in fourth grade, but he must have gotten left . . ."

"Ben and Fred," said Mr. Todd, "I would like that whispering stopped right now."

Ben turned and looked at Steve. Steve was staring right at him, and Steve looked angry.

At recess Ben was playing tag when someone suddenly grabbed his cap. He turned around.

Steve stood there, frowning. "This is a pretty dumb cap, right? Only a chump who whispers about other people would wear a dumb cap like this. Right, chump?"

"Give me back my hat," said Ben.

"Try and get it," sneered Steve. He pushed Ben in the chest.

Suddenly it got very quiet on the
playground. Kids were staring at Ben
and Steve. Ben felt all wobbly inside. He
wanted his cap back, but he didn't want to
fight with Steve.

Then the recess bell rang sharply. Steve turned,
dropped Ben's cap in the dirt, stepped right on it, and
walked back to class.

Ben picked up the hat and dusted it off. "I think
we're in trouble," Fred said.

During arithmetic that afternoon, Mr. Todd asked Steve to multiply 8 times 7. Steve was quiet for a long time. Then he mumbled, "Forty-eight?"

"No, I'm afraid that's not right," said Mr. Todd. "Who does know the answer? How about you, Ben?"

"Fifty-six," Ben answered.

"Good work, Ben," said Mr. Todd.

"Not so good, Ben," whispered Fred. "Steve will really be mad now."

Fred was right. Steve was waiting for Ben after
school. He grabbed Ben's arm and twisted it. "Listen,
'Benjy,'" Steve growled. "Don't you ever try to make
me look stupid in class again."

Fred started jumping around like an excited flea.
"You let Ben go," he yelled, "or there is going to
be trouble."

But Steve just pushed Ben away and ran down the street calling, "Better watch out, chump!"

When Ben got home, his mother asked, "Well, how was the first day of third grade?"

"Okay, I guess," Ben sighed. Then he trudged upstairs.

When Ben got to his room, he flopped onto his bed. Third grade was not going to be neat. It was going to be awful. How could he stop Steve from picking on him? Ben wished that he never had to go back to school again.

Then from a shelf across the room Ben heard a cheery voice.

"Ben, my friend, don't look so sad.
Your luck will change from good to bad.
Just when you think that you're all through,
A Care Bear will come to see you through."
And off the shelf floated a little, green Bear.

"Who are you?" Ben asked.

"My name is Good Luck Bear; hear what I tell.
Don't fight with Steve. All will be well.
Friend Bear will soon come and visit with you.
She can tell you the right thing to do."

Then Good Luck Bear gave a wink, floated out the window and was gone.

What did that Bear mean? Ben wondered. And who was Friend Bear? Ben thought about it until the time he went to bed.

On Tuesday as they walked to school Fred said, "I've been thinking, Ben. And what I think is that the only way for us to get rid of Steve is for you to fight him and beat him. Then he'll leave us alone."

"Easy for you to say," Ben answered. "But *we* are not going to fight. *I* am." He gave a big sigh. "Oh, I don't know what to do, Fred. Last night someone told me that fighting wasn't the answer. And maybe Steve will act differently today."

But at lunch that day Steve bumped into Ben and
made him spill his milk.

And that afternoon Steve tripped Ben during gym class.

Ben began to think that Fred was right.

On Thursday Ben walked home all by himself.
The sky was cold and gray. Ben shivered. He decided
that tomorrow he would have to fight with Steve.

At supper that night Ben said to his father, "Dad, did a bully ever bother you?"

"You bet," his father replied. "He made my life miserable for about a month at the end of fifth grade. But I was lucky. He moved away. Why do you ask? Is everything okay?"

"Oh, yeah, sure," Ben said quickly. He wondered if there was a chance that Steve was getting ready to move. He doubted it.

Ben couldn't get to sleep that night. He tossed and turned. All he could think about was what was going to happen at school the next day.

"I think," said a gentle voice, "that you have a problem."

Ben sat up. There in the moonlight was a small Bear with two daisies on its tummy.

Ben reached out and asked, "Are you Friend Bear?"

"You said it," answered the Bear with a grin. "Careful! I'm a bit ticklish, you know."

Friend Bear floated to the foot of Ben's bed. "Steve's not being very nice, is he?" Friend Bear asked.

"He sure isn't," Ben answered. "What did I ever do to him?"

"Nothing really," said Friend Bear. "But sometimes when people are angry or afraid they hit out at others for no good reason."

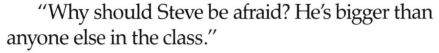

"Why should Steve be afraid? He's bigger than anyone else in the class."

"Maybe that's why he's angry," said Friend Bear. "He's the biggest because he's a year older than anyone else. It's not easy to be left back in school. Does Steve have any good friends in your class?"

"No, not really."

"Well, maybe if someone treated him like a friend, he might turn into a friend."

"Who?"

Friend Bear looked right at Ben and smiled.

"Me?" asked Ben. "How could I? Never!"

Friend Bear said, "Oh, I don't know about that. It might be worth a try."

Then Friend Bear floated off Ben's bed and disappeared into the shadows of the room.

Ben was still thinking about Friend
Bear as he walked to school with Fred the
next day.

"Are you going to fight him today?"
Fred asked anxiously. "Are you scared?"

But Ben just kept thinking as they
walked along, and he didn't say a thing.

That morning in science the class had a discussion about turtles. Steve said that snapping turtles couldn't pull their heads all the way into their shells.

"Are you sure that's right?" asked Mr. Todd.

"It sure is," said Ben. He turned to Steve. "You really know a lot about turtles," he said.

Steve just stared at him.

At lunch that day Ben sat at the far end of the table where Steve always ate. Ben didn't say anything, but when Steve looked at him, Ben smiled.

In gym that afternoon Ben picked Steve to be on his baseball team. After Steve made a good catch, Ben yelled, "Great play, Steve!"

And when Ben hit a triple later in the game, Steve passed him and said quietly, "I guess you're not such a chump after all."

That afternoon Ben and Fred were half way home when they heard Steve's voice. "Hey, you two, come over here."

"Oh, boy," said Fred. "It looks like we're trapped. You'll have to fight for sure now!"

Steve walked up to Ben. "So," he said, "I see
that you are acting nice to me 'cause you're really
scared. Right?"

Ben took a deep breath. "No—no, I'm not," he
said. "And if you want to fight, we will. It's just that I
thought you might like a new friend . . . I know I
would." And Ben put out his hand to shake.

Steve clenched his fists. He glared at Ben for a
long time. Then, slowly, he reached out and shook
Ben's hand. "You're okay," he said.

The next day Steve walked home with Ben and Fred. They stopped for an ice cream cone.

"What I want to know is why you guys didn't fight," said Fred as he licked his cone.

"Oh, I don't know," said Ben with a smile. "Let's just say we had some help from two very good friends."